John Cena

ELBOW GREASE

FAST FRIENDS

JOHN CENA
ELBOW GREASE
FAST FRIENDS

Oooooh, this is gonna be good!

Illustrated by Howard McWilliam

Random House 🏠 New York

When your brothers are monster trucks,
they tend to play rough.

Especially when they're faster

or smarter

Elbow Grease needed a break from playing with Flash, Crash, Pinball, and Tank. Mel the mechanic invited him to go to the junkyard to look for spare parts.

The junkyard was sprawling, stuffed with discarded parts and broken-down machines. To Elbow Grease, it seemed like a dump. To Mel, it was the most exciting place in the whole world. She dug through the junk piles with her shovel as if hunting for treasure.

Elbow Grease went off to explore. He climbed to the top of the highest heap of junk—and that's when he saw it.

In a far corner of the junkyard, a sleek two-wheeled vehicle whipped, flipped, and twirled through a scrap-tacular stunt course made from scrunched-up chunks of metal, pools of broken glass, and tangles of razor wire.

The gleaming purple monster-cycle was named Chopper. When she finished training, she noticed she had an audience.

Mel was clapping so hard her hands hurt, and Elbow Grease felt a little jealous.

Mel was flabbergasted. It was better than anything she had ever built.

Chopper recognized Elbow Grease from the King of the Crud videos she had seen online.

Mel invited Chopper back to the Demolition Derby to meet the whole team. 'Bo carried the spare parts Mel had collected and followed as close behind as he could.

At first, the trucks were impressed with Chopper's speed, skill, strength, and style. But their enthusiasm didn't last long.

Catch me if you can, boys!

Chopper was faster than Flash.

Hurry up!

She drives like a maniac!

Chopper was smarter than Pinball.

Gotcha!

She's cheating!

Chopper was more daring than Crash.

And, despite being smaller, Chopper was tougher than Tank.

The monster trucks were frustrated. They weren't used to losing.

We don't want to play anymore!

Elbow Grease was shocked.

WHAAAT? No plug?!

Mel was impressed.

Wow, induction charging. Wish I'd thought of that!

After lunch, Chopper could tell something was bothering her new friend.

Anything wrong? Maybe I can help. I'm pretty good at solving problems.

You think you're good at everything! That's why no one likes playing with you!

Insecurity surged through Elbow Grease's circuits, and he shouted before thinking about his words.

Chopper was hurt. She raced out of the garage without saying a word.

Chopper! Wait!

Mel threw her hands in the air and began shouting.

That's because when I see someone do better than me, I feel motivated to work harder. It's a little something called gumption. Ever heard of it?

Elbow Grease was embarrassed, and his brothers realized that Mel was right. They decided to go apologize to Chopper.

Back at the junkyard, Chopper had never felt more alone. She thought she had finally made some friends, but then she acted like a show-off and pushed them away. She was so frustrated that she began to destroy her beautiful stunt course.

As Chopper crashed and smashed through the scraps, she knocked loose the base of the giant junkyard crane.

She was shouting too loudly to hear the terrible creak as the crane began to fall.

I don't care if I ever have a friend! I'll do it all alone! I don't need anyone's help!

The falling crane scraped and sparked against Elbow Grease's bumper as he shoved Chopper out of the way at the very last second.

Mel and the trucks helped Chopper put the junkyard back in order.

THE END

Visit us on the Web! rhcbooks.com
Educators and librarians, for a variety of teaching tools, visit us at RHTeachersLibrarians.com

Library of Congress Cataloging-in-Publication Data
Names: Cena, John, author. | McWilliam, Howard, illustrator.
Title: Fast Friends / John Cena ; illustrated by Howard McWilliam.
Description: New York : Random House, [2020] | Series: Elbow Grease |
Audience: Ages 3–7. | Audience: Grades K–1. | Summary: Monster truck
Elbow Grease and his brothers meet a monster-cycle, Chopper, and hope to
be her friend—until she proves to be faster, smarter, and more capable
than they are.
Identifiers: LCCN 2019054382 (print) | LCCN 2019054383 (ebook) |
ISBN 978-0-593-17934-5 (hardcover) | ISBN 978-0-593-17935-2 (library binding) |
ISBN 978-0-593-17936-9 (ebook)
Subjects: LCSH: Motorcycles—Fiction. | CYAC: Monster trucks—Fiction. |
Trucks—Fiction. | Ability—Fiction. | Brothers—Fiction.
Classification: LCC PZ7.1.C4648 Fas 2020 (print) |
LCC PZ7.1.C4648 (ebook) | DDC [E]—dc23

MANUFACTURED IN CHINA
10 9 8 7 6 5 4 3 2 1
First Edition